Jenny

PUFFIN BOOKS

Crocodile Cana

Angie Sage lives in Bristol and ha̶ daughters aged fourteen and nineteen. She studi̶ d illustration at Leicester Polytechnic and since the̶ has illustrated many children's books. She started ̶riting nine years ago and now writes and illustra̶es for ages three to ten. When Angie Sage is not w̶it̶ng or drawing, she likes walking along a Cornish beach and watching the sea.

ther books by Angie Sage

ALLIE'S CROCODILE

SHARK ISLAND

ready, steady, read!

THE LITTLE GREEN BOOK OF
THE LAST LOST DINOSAURS

THE LITTLE PINK BOOK OF THE
WOOLLY MAMMOTH

Angie Sage

Crocodile Canal

PUFFIN BOOKS

For the ~~19/0~~ 2003
Middlesex Hospital Radiography set,
not forgetting Miss Frank

PUFFIN BOOKS

Published by the Penguin Group
Penguin Books Ltd, 27 Wrights Lane, London W8 5TZ, England
Penguin Putnam Inc., 375 Hudson Street, New York, New York 10014, USA
Penguin Books Australia Ltd, Ringwood, Victoria, Australia
Penguin Books Canada Ltd, 10 Alcorn Avenue, Toronto, Ontario, Canada M4V 3B2
Penguin Books (NZ) Ltd, 182–190 Wairau Road, Auckland 10, New Zealand

Penguin Books Ltd, Registered Offices: Harmondsworth, Middlesex, England

First published 1998
1 3 5 7 9 10 8 6 4 2

Copyright © Angie Sage, 1998
All rights reserved

The moral right of the author/illustrator has been asserted

Filmset in Baskerville MT

Made and printed in England by Clays Ltd, St Ives plc

British Library Cataloguing in Publication Data
A CIP catalogue record for this book is available from the British Library

ISBN 0–140–38949–0

Chapter 1

"JUST WHIZZ IT around a couple of times and then let go," said Gran as she handed Allie a large haddock. "That's what I do. You'd be surprised how far it goes."

Allie took the haddock and whizzed it round really fast. Gran was right, the haddock flew high up in the air and landed with a loud splash at the far side of the lake.

"Good shot," said Gran. "Here he comes now."

Gran and Allie were standing on the bank of the lake in Gran's back garden.

It was a new lake which Gran had had dug a few months earlier, and only Allie knew the real reason why. It was a secret between Allie and Gran. They stood together on the bank and watched the secret glide through the water towards the haddock. SNAP! The haddock was gone.

Gran wiped her hands on her apron. "Well," she said, "that's the last one. Although he'll still be hungry, you wait and see."

"But he's had a whole bucketful, Gran," said Allie. "He can't possibly want any more fish."

"Oh yes he can," muttered Gran as she gazed at a stream of bubbles making their way towards her. Two crocodile eyes and a long crocodile nose surfaced at Gran's feet.

"Got any more fish, Gran?" the crocodile asked.

"No," said Gran.

"Oh. Not even a little one?"

"No," said Gran firmly.

The crocodile pulled himself out of the water and lay on the bank beside Allie and Gran.

"Well, I'll just have my nap then." He settled down on the grass and slowly closed his eyes.

Allie looked at the crocodile. She remembered the day she had found him by a parking meter. It was not so very

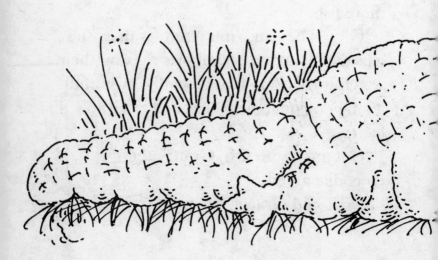

long ago, but he had looked different then, he had looked more . . . thin.

"Gran," said Allie, "he's getting fat."

The crocodile's eyes opened. "*Fat?* I am not fat. How very rude. I shall have my nap elsewhere." He got up and slowly waddled off.

"Oops," said Allie. "I thought he was asleep."

"Never mind, dear, he'll get over it." Gran looked at the chubby crocodile

settling down underneath the apple tree. "Anyway, you're right. He *is* fat. He eats too much and hardly swims at all. Whenever I look out of the window he's just floating around like an old log."

"Perhaps you should put some more fish in the lake, Gran," suggested Allie. "You know, like you did when the lake was new. Then he'd have to catch them himself."

"That was a whole truckload I had poured into the lake and he ate the lot in three days," said Gran. "No, he needs more exercise. I've tried getting out of the rubber dinghy and making him chase me round the lake, and I've even thrown sticks for him to catch, but he just gives me one of his funny looks and goes to sleep."

Gran picked up the empty fish-bucket and Allie followed her indoors. Gran put the bucket down beside the huge fish-freezer, which took up half the kitchen.

"Well, dear," she said thoughtfully, taking off her apron. "I'll walk you home now. I promised your mum you'd be back for tea today. I do believe I've got something to ask her too."

"What's that then, Gran?"

Gran raised her eyebrows in the way she always did when she had a secret. "Wait and see, dear. But even if I do say so myself, this is one of my better ideas. I think we can all have fun and that chubby crocodile can lose weight at the same time."

Allie hopped around excitedly. "What is it, Gran? Come on, Gran, tell me!"

"I have to ask your mum first. Then I might tell you – if you're good."

"Oh, *Gran*," protested Allie. But Gran just smiled mysteriously.

Chapter 2

"HI, MUM," SAID Allie as she followed
Gran into the sitting room. Allie stopped
suddenly. Sitting on the sofa was a thin
girl who looked strangely familiar. She
had piercing little blue eyes and a thin,
sharp nose. She sat very still and upright
with her bony knees pressed tightly
together. She stared hard at Allie. Allie
stared hard back.

"Allie, this is Arabella Python," said
Mum.

Allie jumped as though a large spider
had run down her neck. Her mum gave
her a funny look and carried on.

"Arabella and her mother, Demelza, are staying with her Uncle Ernest. You know her uncle, Allie. He's that nice Mr Python next door, who works in the reptile house at the zoo."

Allie knew Mr Python only too well. Mr Python had come very close to guessing that Gran was looking after the crocodile. In fact, Mr Python was one of the reasons why the crocodile had gone to live with Gran instead of staying with Allie.

"Well, Allie," said her mum rather crossly, "you might try saying 'hello' to Arabella, who has kindly said that she can play with you this afternoon."

Allie stared at the carpet. "Hello," she mumbled.

Arabella sprang up from the sofa and skipped over to Allie.

"I am *so* pleased to meet you at last," she trilled. "My darling uncle has told me so much about you –" Allie made her

sickbag face at Gran "– and your *wonderful* granny. I'd love to see the lake in her back garden. I'm sure there are *interesting* things in it."

Allie's mum laughed. "Oh, I don't think so, Arabella. Gran tried keeping fish, but they all disappeared. Now all she has is a mouldy old log floating around. Very unsavoury if you ask me." Allie's mum gave a polite giggle. "Now, let's all go and

have tea. Come on, Allie, show your guest
the way to the kitchen."

For someone so thin, Arabella eats a lot
of food, thought Allie. She ploughed her
way through all Allie's favourite egg
sandwiches and then got started on the
chocolate cake. Gran managed to grab
the last piece just in time. She popped it
on to Allie's plate.

"Thanks, Gran," whispered Allie. "Are

you going to ask Mum about, you know, your *idea*?"

"It's rude to whisper," piped up Arabella.

"What? Oh, yes," mumbled Gran through a chocolate digestive.

"Go on then, Gran."

"Oh, Susan dear –" started Gran. Allie tried not to giggle. She always thought it was funny when she heard Gran talking to her mum as though Mum was a little girl.

Gran carried on. "I think, Susan, that it would be nice for Allie if I took her on a little holiday next week. We fancy a trip along the canal on one of those lovely old barges, don't we, Allie?"

"Do we?" Allie was surprised. She'd had a guess at all kinds of things, but she hadn't thought it might be a canal trip. "Oh, yes," said Allie quickly, "we do. Definitely."

Allie's mum did not look too pleased about this. "Oh, that's a shame," she said, "now that Arabella is here and you have a little friend to play with, Allie."

"But, *Mum* . . ." protested Allie. "You

can't let Gran go on holiday on her own. She needs me to go and help her with the boat. Don't you, Gran?"

"Oh yes," said Gran. "I couldn't manage on my own. Not at all."

Allie's mum looked at Gran. She had a strange feeling that there was more to the holiday than she realized.

"Please, Mum," said Allie.

"All right, Allie," said Mum. "It's just a shame that you'll miss most of Arabella's stay."

Suddenly, Arabella piped up, "Actually, Mrs Jones, I won't be available to play with Allie for the next two weeks. I too am going away with my mother and Uncle Ernest. So I am sure it would be all right for little Allie to have a holiday with her granny."

Allie stared at Arabella. She wanted to give her a hefty kick, but she stuck out her tongue instead. Arabella stuck both

her fingers up her nose and went cross-eyed.

"Don't do that, dear," said Gran to Arabella. "The wind might change and then you'd be stuck like that for ever."

Allie smiled. She didn't care about Arabella. She was already feeling excited about her week on the canal with Gran and the crocodile.

Chapter 3

IT WAS VERY early the next Saturday morning when Gran drove a small white van up to the canal. She carefully parked the van some way away from a little hut that stood by the canal lock. There was a big sign on the hut that read BOAT HIRE.

Gran opened the doors at the back of the van. "Come on, you two, out you get!"

"I can't feel my tail," grumbled the crocodile. "It's gone to sleep. You could have hired a bigger van, Gran."

"Come *on*, get out," Allie told the

crocodile. She was longing to see the boat
that Gran had hired for their week's
holiday.

"It's all very well for you. You haven't
had someone sitting on your tail for ages,"
the crocodile muttered as he tried to turn
round.

"I haven't got a tail," said Allie.

"Exactly."

Allie and Gran helped the crocodile out of the van and then heaved out their bags.

The crocodile stood on the bank of the canal and gazed at the water. "Lovely," he murmured. "Haven't seen so much water since my river." He gave a sigh. "Well, time for a swim!"

"*Not yet, dear,*" whispered Gran, who suddenly felt worried. She hadn't thought about this bit – about how to get the crocodile on to the canal boat without being seen.

"*Daisy May!*" yelled Allie.

"Shh," tutted Gran. "What *do* you mean, Allie?"

"Our boat. You remember, Gran. You said our boat was called the *Daisy May*. There it is!" Allie pointed to a long, narrow canal boat, brightly painted in red and green. She thought it looked lovely, bobbing on the water in the misty early morning sunshine.

The crocodile peered in the direction that Allie was pointing. "Boat?" he said. "What d'you want a boat for when there's all this lovely water?"

"We're going on a canal holiday in a boat," explained Allie. "Gran told you last night."

"Did she? I don't remember."

"I wondered if you were asleep," said Gran. "Sometimes it's hard to tell. Look, Allie, why don't you both slip on to the *Daisy May* while I go and sort things out over there." With that, Gran trotted off to the BOAT-HIRE hut.

Allie jumped on to the *Daisy May*. "Come on then," she said to the crocodile. The crocodile looked at Allie as though she had said something stupid. "How?" he said.

"Oh," said Allie. In the distance she saw

Gran come out of the hut with the boatman. They started walking over towards the *Daisy May*. Allie grabbed hold of an old plank that was lying on the flat roof of the *Daisy May*.

"Quick, get on to this!" she said, and swung the plank over. It banged down in front of the crocodile. "Mind my feet," he muttered. Carefully, the crocodile shuffled up the plank and slipped into the boat.

Allie could hear Gran talking to the boat owner as they wandered over. They were getting very close and the crocodile was easy to see. In fact his tail was hanging over the side of the boat. Allie threw open the two little doors that led into the long, narrow cabin of the boat. "Come on," she said to the crocodile. "Let's have a look in here."

The crocodile went in. Allie waited until all of his tail was inside the cabin, then she jumped after him and slammed the doors shut. She was just in time – moments later the *Daisy May* rocked as Gran and the boatman came on board.

"Here's the keys. You'll find she's a lovely boat. Just take it slow to begin with," the boatman was saying to Gran.

The crocodile followed Allie through the main cabin, which had two long seats and a table. At one end was a little kitchen with a small sink and a cooker. A narrow

corridor took them further along the
boat, where they found two smaller
cabins. Allie pushed open a door and saw
two bunk beds and a tiny, painted
cupboard.

"Isn't this sweet?" she said to the
crocodile. "I'll have the top bunk and you
have the bottom bunk."

Allie climbed up and lay stretched out
on the top bunk. There was a porthole in

just the right place. She could look out and see everything that was happening. In fact, as she looked she saw a large red car pull up outside the BOAT-HIRE hut. Allie had the strange feeling she had seen that car somewhere before.

THUMP! Down in the bottom bunk the crocodile was making himself comfortable. Allie leaned over the edge of her bunk and looked down at him.

"Do you like it then?" she asked.

The crocodile looked at her thoughtfully. "Well," he said, "I don't know about floating on water when you could have a perfectly good swim in it, but if you're going to float around, you may as well do it in something that is crocodile-shaped."

"Crocodile-shaped?" asked Allie.

"Yes. Long and narrow. Like me."

"I don't know about *narrow*," muttered Allie.

"What did you say?"

"Er – nothing."

"I am *not* fat," said the crocodile grumpily, and he stomped off to find Gran.

Chapter 4

THE CROCODILE WAS leaning over the side of the boat while Gran tried to start the engine for what felt like the hundredth time. He gazed longingly at the brown water of the canal. Allie was sitting on the flat roof of the boat, watching the people from the red car. They were banging on the door of the BOAT-HIRE hut. There were three of them: one thin person wearing amazingly bright, orange trousers, one shorter fat person in a huge pink dress, and a small noisy one. The boatman came out and the people barged into his hut. The door slammed.

What horrible people, thought Allie.

Gran sat down next to the crocodile. "It won't start," she sighed. "When the boatman's finished with those people I'll ask him what to do."

The crocodile looked puzzled. "What about this boat-thing's legs then . . . or flippers? Don't they work?"

"It doesn't have any." Gran smiled.

"Of course it does, Gran. I'll just nip in

and have a quick look. I'll sort it out for
you." Before Gran could say anything, the
crocodile heaved himself over the side of
the boat and dropped into the water with
a loud splash.

"No! Come back!" shouted Gran, but
the crocodile had disappeared. "Oh,
Allie," said Gran. "He is silly sometimes."

Allie did not reply. She was still looking
at the BOAT-HIRE hut. Suddenly the

door flew open and the three horrible people marched out with the boatman trotting behind them. They were making for the much bigger blue boat that was moored just behind the *Daisy May*.

Allie stared as they drew closer. It can't be, it *can't* be, she thought. It can be. *It is.* It's the *Pythons*. *Oh no!*

Allie jumped down from the roof. Arabella looked towards her and waved. "All-ieee. Coo-eee!" she trilled. Allie ran towards the engine key and turned it hard. Nothing happened, but to her surprise the *Daisy May* started to move anyway. Allie slipped off the mooring rope, grabbed the helm and steered the barge out into the middle of the canal.

"Allie – what *are* you doing, dear?" asked Gran as the barge silently floated along with the current.

"We've got to go, Gran. Look who's here!" Allie pointed at the Pythons.

"Oh my. Oh dearie, dearie, dear," whispered Gran. "That revolting little Python man. He's after the crocodile. I'll bet that nosy Arabella has told him about this. Allie, how come we're moving? The engine isn't going."

The crocodile popped his head out of the water.

"Ah, Gran . . . This boat thing . . . It doesn't have any flippers . . . Not

surprising it won't go . . . got to push
it . . ." He seemed out of breath.

Gran peered over the side. "Keep your
head down or that Python man will see
you," she said in a loud whisper. "I'll try
the engine again."

Gran tried the engine. This time it
started. The *Daisy May* sped up and the
crocodile paddled furiously behind. "Hey,
wait for me," he puffed.

Allie stared back at the big blue Python boat. The Pythons were busy loading up. Ernest Python carried a long green bag on board. It was probably a good thing that Allie was too far away to read the words on the side of the bag. They said:

KATCH-A-KROC KIT
The smart way to catch a crocodile

Chapter 5

THE *DAISY MAY* chugged as fast as she could go along the canal. A cross crocodile caught up with her.

"It's rude to leave crocodiles behind," he puffed indignantly.

Gran looked at the crocodile swimming along through the greeny-brown water. He was almost the same colour as the water and not at all easy to see, but Gran knew that Ernest Python could spot a crocodile in a canal with his eyes closed.

"We'd better get the crocodile on board quick," Gran said to Allie. "That Python man will be after him before you can say 'zoo'."

"Shh, Gran," whispered Allie, "don't upset him."

"I'll jolly well upset his whole silly boat if he comes any closer," grumbled Gran.

"I mean don't upset the *crocodile*," said

Allie. She leaned over the side of the boat. "Can you get in the boat now?" she asked. "Quickly?"

"No," said the crocodile. He bobbed around, just about keeping pace with the *Daisy May*. He was having the nicest swim he'd had for a very long time. He did not want to get out.

"It's important," said Allie. "Please?"

The crocodile looked up at Allie. She was about a metre above him. He looked up at the boat thing, which he knew had no flippers at all, no legs and no tail. It did not even have any scales that a crocodile could hang on to.

"How exactly", he asked Allie, "am I supposed to get all the way up there?"

Before Allie could think of an answer Gran grabbed her. She pointed behind them. Coming around the bend was the Pythons' boat. It was fast.

"Oh my goodness me! Oh, Allie, they're

catching up with us!" gabbled Gran.

Gran was right, the big blue Python boat was getting nearer and nearer. Gran and Allie could hear the noise of its powerful engines as it thundered towards the *Daisy May*. They could even hear Arabella squawking "Yoo-hoo! We're be*hind* you!"

"Faster!" said Allie. "We've got to go faster!" They were coming up to a very sharp bend in the canal. Desperately Allie grabbed hold of the tiller and pulled hard on the throttle. The boat sped up.

"Oi!" shouted the crocodile. "Wait for me!"

"No," yelled Gran. "You get those legs going and keep up. Come on now – one two three four, one two three four!"

The boat swung into the bend and the crocodile puffed along behind. A small boy on the canal bank stared with wide open eyes. "Hey, Dad,' he yelped, "there's

a boat being chased by a crocodile."
"That's nice, James," said his dad as he
tried to read the Saturday paper.

The bend was sharper than Allie
expected and the *Daisy May* was going
faster than she was used to. Just for a
moment, Allie panicked and clumsily
pushed the tiller the wrong way. The

Daisy May swung sharply across the bend and kept on going. She was now pointing at the other side of the canal and heading straight towards a huge clump of dense bushes on the opposite bank. Gran screamed. Allie closed her eyes and waited for the crash.

There wasn't one. There was a loud scratching sound as the tops of the bushes

swept over the shiny black paint of the *Daisy May*'s roof. Gran and Allie ducked down as the bushes twanged over their heads and got snagged in their hair. Allie dared to open her eyes, and to her amazement the *Daisy May* was still gliding through water. The bushes had closed up behind them and in front of them was a beautiful, silent and deserted cutting.

"Turn the engine off," whispered Gran. They drifted quietly forwards and bumped up against a submerged log.

"Ouch!" said the crocodile.

"Shh," said Gran. "Listen . . ." They listened. They heard the Pythons' boat zoom past the hidden cutting and go on its way up the canal.

"Phew, that was close," said Gran.

Chapter 6

ALLIE WAS SITTING on a shady bank in
the deserted cutting, happily dabbling
her toes in the water. Gran was lying on
the roof of the *Daisy May* quietly reading
her book. The boat rocked gently as
small waves from a diving crocodile
lapped up against the sides. It was the
most peaceful place that Allie had ever
known, with the sun shining through the
trees and casting dancing shadows on the
quiet water. The only sound was the
splash of the crocodile's tail as he
swooped down through the cool canal
water.

"Let's have some lunch, Gran," said Allie.

"You could set up the barbecue," said Gran. "Then I'll light it. OK?"

"Great!" said Allie. She scrambled on to the *Daisy May* and found the barbecue stashed in one of the little cupboards below the tiny sink. Allie loved the way everything was so small in the *Daisy May*, it was just right for someone her size.

While Allie fiddled around on the bank with the barbecue, the crocodile was getting hungry too. He had spent a long time hanging around on the mud at the bottom of the canal, waiting to see if any interesting fish came his way, but he had seen no fish at all. Then he had just missed a small water rat because he had been scratching his tummy at the time. At last he snapped at a fat water snake. It had stuck to his teeth and tasted like old rubber, but at least it was food. He took it up to the surface to give it a good shake.

"Eurgh!" said Allie. "What are you doing with that horrible old bike tyre?"

The crocodile spat it out in disgust. "Well," he said, "it's a good thing we're having lunch soon. I'm starving. There's nothing in this canal to keep an athletic young crocodile going." He wandered off and settled down for a sleep in some long grass. Allie threw the slimy old bike tyre back into the canal.

Allie and Gran watched the sausages and burgers sizzle above the glowing charcoal. When they were ready, Gran made them each a burger in a bun. Allie sprayed tomato ketchup all over her burger and took a huge bite. "Mmm-mmm-mmm . . . ooh, Gran, this tastes fantastic."

Over in the long grass the crocodile opened his eyes and sniffed the air.

"Lunch." he said. "About time too." He got up and walked over happily to join Allie and Gran.

Allie saw him coming. "Hey, Gran, you've forgotten his lunch."

"No I haven't," said Gran.

"But where is it then?" asked Allie, who remembered that she hadn't even seen Gran bring any fish on to the boat. In fact Allie now realized why Gran had looked different that day. She hadn't been carrying fish. Ever since the crocodile had arrived, Allie had rarely seen Gran without a haddock in her pocket or a piece of cod in her bag. But today Gran had been completely *fish-free*.

"His lunch is in the canal," said Gran with her mouth full.

"Excuse me, Gran," the crocodile put his head on one side and gave Gran a long, crocodile stare, "my lunch is *where*?"

"In the canal, dear. There are some

lovely fresh fish there. It will do you good
to catch your own food while we're on
holiday. You'll get lots of exercise, and
fresh fish will be so much better for you
than your usual frozen stuff."

The crocodile looked amazed. "What
about pudding then?" he said.

"That's in the canal too, dear," said
Gran as she started on a hot dog.

Allie gazed at the crocodile from behind
her burger. She wondered how he was
going to take this. Not well, she thought.
She was right. The crocodile snapped his
teeth together, turned around and did a
huge bellyflop into the canal. Half the
canal landed on the barbecue. The other
half washed away what was left of Gran's
hot dog.

"Well," sighed Gran, "at least we don't
have to wash up now. Don't go looking at
me like that, Allie. It's for his own good.

Fresh fish are much better for him and he'll lose that fat tummy of his if he has to swim and catch them too. That was the whole point of coming on this holiday. It's his own fitness programme."

"I know, Gran," said Allie. "But I'm not sure if he sees it like that. Anyway, I'm glad I don't have to catch my burgers in the canal."

The crocodile was cross. He swooped down after a small baby water rat which escaped into its burrow in the nick of time. The water rat was kept in for the rest of the afternoon for telling fibs about crocodiles, but two elderly water rats out for an afternoon swim were not quite so lucky.

Chapter 7

IT'S HARD TO get to sleep when there's a crocodile sulking on your bedroom roof. It's even harder when the crocodile's tummy is rumbling. Loudly.

Allie tossed and turned inside her sleeping bag, but every time she began to drop off to sleep there was another loud gurgle and she woke up again. So she was very surprised when it was suddenly morning and Gran poked her head around the narrow door. "Toast?" asked Gran.

Allie sat and munched her toast while Gran steered the *Daisy May* out of the cutting.

"Those dratted Pythons will be well ahead by now," said Gran. "We can just tootle along and enjoy our holiday." The *Daisy May* pushed her way back through the bushes.

"Hee hee hee, oh, *don't*. Oh, ha ha ha!" The crocodile was rolling around on the roof of the *Daisy May* as the bushes brushed over him.

"Well," said Gran to Allie, "who would

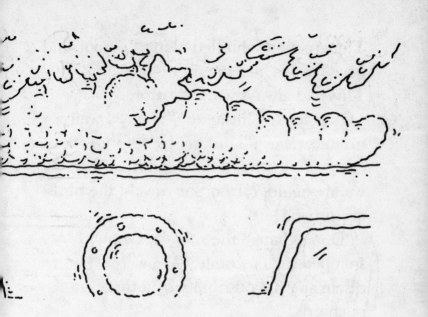

have thought that a crocodile would be
ticklish? At least he seems in a better
mood this morning."

"I am not in a better mood," said the
crocodile. "I am absolutely starving.
There's no fish in this canal, Gran."

"There must be, dear . . ."

"I tell you, Gran, I'm so hungry I'd eat
anything swimming in this canal. Haven't
you got even a small tin of pilchards?"

The crocodile shuffled along the roof and gave her his 'just one more fish' look. This had always worked before.

Gran looked flustered. "Um . . . wait a minute, dear. I'll just get us out into the canal . . . left hand down a bit . . . here we are again, off on our travels, the birds are singing –"

"Don't change the subject, Gran," snapped the crocodile. "We were discussing the possibility of a tin of pilchards."

Allie swallowed her last mouthful of toast. "Oh, go on, Gran, let him have a tin of pilchards. He'll be too weak to catch any fish if you don't."

"Well, I'm glad someone here understands the crocodile digestion," said the crocodile.

Gran looked unhappy. "I'm sorry, dear. I really didn't bring any fish at all. I'm sure you'll find some in the canal today."

The crocodile snorted in disgust. "Rubbish," he said. "That's all there is in this canal. Rubbish and rats. They both taste revolting." He closed his eyes and went to sleep. Every now and then his tummy gave a long, crocodile gurgle.

The *Daisy May* chuntered on along the canal. Allie sat next to the crocodile and gazed at the water flowing past. Gran scanned the canal bank as they drifted by. She seemed to be looking for something. It wasn't long before she found it.

"A proper loo!" shouted Gran as a noisy campsite appeared round the next bend.

"What?" asked Allie.

"I don't like the funny one in the boat. I'll just nip into the campsite here and borrow their loo," Gran said rather loudly in the direction of the crocodile. Then she whispered to Allie, "Those campsites always have a shop. I thought I'd just get

him a little tin of pilchards. Only one, mind."

Gran steered the *Daisy May* along the bank and tied up on a post. In a moment she was disappearing through a tall gate that led into the busy campsite. A crowd of children gathered and started pointing at the crocodile.

"Hey, look at that blow-up crocodile."

"I've got a better one than that."

"That's nothing like a *real* crocodile."

"Yeah, it's too fat."

Allie saw the crocodile's tail twitch. "Shh," she whispered. "You've got to keep still."

A bossy woman in a yellow blazer, wearing a big badge which said *Kiddie Kamper Klub – I'm Katie*, homed in on the children.

"Now, now, Kiddie Kampers, what are you doing here?" she trilled. "It's time for Uncle Peter's puppet show."

The children groaned. "Oh no. Not again."

"Now, now, Kiddie Kampers. Ooh, who left this gate open? We don't want any Kiddie Kampers in the canal, do we?"

The children groaned again and trooped back into the campsite. Katie Kiddie Kamper Klub locked the gate.

Oh, crumbs, thought Allie. What's Gran going to do?

What Gran did was rattle the gate very hard and then try to climb over the fence. She piled up three old milk crates and clambered on top of them. She was fine until the milk crates started to wobble and she grabbed the top of the fence just as they all fell over. Gran was left hanging on to the top of the fence.

"Help," she said.

Allie rushed over but there was nothing she could do. "You'll have to let go, Gran," she said.

"I can't let go," said Gran. "I'll fall. And I'll be stuck in this horrid campsite."

"You could always go and watch Uncle Peter's puppet show," giggled Allie.

"That's not funny, Allie."

"That's what the Kiddie Kampers thought too –"

"Excuse me, Gran," interrupted the crocodile, "may I be of any assistance?" He didn't wait for an answer, but slid

through the bars of the gate into the
campsite. A few moments later Allie saw a
crocodile nose appear and suddenly Gran
was sitting on top of the fence.

"Stay there, Gran," the crocodile told her.

"I don't think I can do anything else,
dear," said Gran nervously. The crocodile
slipped back through the gate and stood
right up on his tail so that he easily
reached Gran. He held out his two

stumpy front legs and lifted Gran down from the top of the fence.

"Thank you so much, dear," puffed Gran as she clambered back on to the *Daisy May*.

"My pleasure, Gran," said the crocodile. "Glad to be able to help." His tummy gave a loud gurgle.

"That reminds me." Gran smiled. She fished around in her pockets.

"Yes?" The crocodile looked interested. His tummy gave another gurgle.

"They didn't have any pilchards, so I got you these. Just to stop your tummy rumbling." Gran pulled out a bag of sweets. She emptied them on to the deck. They were fish-shaped jellies.

"Oh," said the crocodile as he scooped up the jelly fish. "Ah. Hmm. Thank you, Gran. Very interesting. Funny how they stick to your teeth. Just like that rubber snake."

Then he dived back into the canal to look for fish – and to clean his teeth.

Chapter 8

ONE OLD BOOT, two pram wheels and a slimy something lay on the deck of the *Daisy May*. They were beginning to smell. Gran sniffed. "He's doing it on purpose," she declared. "Of course there are fish in the canal, he just doesn't want to catch them."

Part of a car tyre came sailing through the air and landed in front of Allie. The crocodile poked his head out of the water.

"*You* try and eat that," he said crossly. He flicked his tail and dived back under the water.

The *Daisy May* chugged along quietly.

Allie read her book and Gran steered the
narrow boat along the peaceful canal.
Time passed in a quiet, dreamlike way
until Gran said, "Where is he, by the
way?" Allie listened. She realized that she
hadn't heard the tell-tale splash of a
diving crocodile for quite a while. Gran
looked over the side of the boat.

"I can't see him anywhere, Allie." She
sounded worried. "Where has he got to . . .

oh my goodness, Allie, can you hear what I can hear?"

Allie could hear only too well. Loud piercing screams echoed ahead of them. "EEIIE! AAH – HELP, HELP!"

"You don't think it's him, do you?" asked Gran.

"Well, he said he was starving . . . he said he'd eat *anything* swimming in the canal . . ."

"Oh *no*! Allie, he *wouldn't*, would he . . . he wouldn't eat a *person*?" Gran speeded up the *Daisy May*.

The screams got louder as the *Daisy May* reached a sharp bend in the canal. Allie rushed to the front of the boat and as the *Daisy May* rounded the bend she saw a crowded café on the canal bank. There was a throng of people clustered along the edge of the bank and someone was screaming, "My baby! My baby! MY BABY'S IN THE WATER!"

Allie, who had her life-saver's certificate, did not think twice. She pulled off her shoes, took a deep breath and dived into the cold, muddy canal water.

Chapter 9

IT WAS COLD and black under the water.
Cold, black and scary. Allie opened her
eyes, but it made no difference – it was
still black. It was still cold and scary too.
Allie had dived deep and she soon hit the
bottom of the canal. It was thick, slimy
mud. She turned and kicked to go up
again but her foot got caught in
something that felt like a shopping trolley.
Allie wriggled and twisted in the darkness,
she pulled and tugged but her foot would
not come free.

I mustn't panic . . . I mustn't breathe . . .
but . . . I've *got* . . . to breathe, thought

69

Allie. Something cold and scaly brushed against her. Allie opened her mouth to scream but shut it again as the gritty canal water poured in. The cold, scaly thing nudged her foot out of the shopping trolley and Allie shot up to the surface like a cork out of a bottle, spluttering and choking.

"You want to watch out for dose shopping trolleys," said the crocodile in a strangely muffled voice. "I got by tail stuck in one. Are you all right?"

Allie gasped. "Oh yes . . . oh, thank you . . ."

"Do you think you could let go of by dose then, please?"

Allie let go. "Sorry. I just needed to hold on to something for a moment."

A piercing scream tore through the air. "MY BABEEE!" Allie remembered why she had jumped into the canal.

"There's a baby in the canal, we've got

to get it out," she told the crocodile.

"Just climb on," he said. "I'll stay underneath the water and they'll all think it's you swimming." Allie clambered on to the crocodile and he took off through the water like a torpedo. The crowd that had gathered on the edge of the bank gasped as Allie came swishing past. She cut through the water like a speedboat and headed towards a splashing figure in the middle of a wide stretch of the canal.

The figure was screeching and kicking and generally making a lot of fuss. Allie thought it looked pretty big for a baby.

"Ooh," went the crowd as Allie zoomed towards it.

"Aah," gasped the crowd as Allie hauled the 'baby' out and sat it on the crocodile. Then it was Allie's turn to gasp.

The 'baby' was Arabella Python.

Chapter 10

ARABELLA PYTHON WAS not a bit
grateful. Allie and the crocodile took her
safely across to the agitated crowd on the
bank. The crocodile kept well below the
water so that no one could see him, but
Arabella was not fooled.

"We're sitting on a crocodile," she hissed
at Allie. "My uncle *said* you and your
Gran had a croco – mnff." Suddenly a
huge pink towel landed on the dripping
Arabella, and Demelza howled, "My
baby! My baby's been saved!" Demelza
swept Arabella up into her arms and
carried her off through the crowd.

The crowd gathered around Allie talking excitedly.

"Such a brave little girl . . ."

"None of us could swim, you see . . ."

"Never seen anyone swim so fast . . ."

But Allie pushed past them. She was going straight back to the *Daisy May*. Allie knew that if Demelza and Arabella Python were at the café, then Ernest Python was there too. And that meant that Ernest Python was close to the crocodile. She and Gran had to get away before Ernest Python found the crocodile.

But where was the *Daisy May*? Allie knew she had to find it. Fast.

Allie had just pushed her way past the last admiring onlooker when she saw a sight she most definitely did not want to see. Arabella was talking to Ernest Python. There was no mistaking Ernest in his fluorescent orange trousers.

Arabella was talking about the crocodile. Allie watched her as she stretched out her stick-like arms to show how long the crocodile was and she made snapping movements with her hands. Ernest Python looked more excited than Allie had ever seen him. He was nodding like one of those toy dogs you get in the back of car windows. Then he clapped his hands together and rushed away.

Allie gasped. She and Gran had to get away with the crocodile. Now. But *still* she could not see where the *Daisy May* was. And where was Gran? Allie turned to run, but with a soft, pink thump she ran straight into Demelza Python.

"Oh, look, Arabella," whinnied Demelza with delight. "Here's the lovely little Allie who rescued you. What a *coincidence* you being on holiday here too, Allie. And *such* a fast swimmer." Arabella made snapping crocodile movements at Allie behind Demelza's back.

Allie said nothing. She tried to push past Demelza, but Demelza's fat, pink arm snaked around her and held her fast. She was trapped in her python-like grip.

"Now, Allie," cooed Demelza, "you must come and have a nice fizzy drink with us." She saw Allie's face. "You don't like fizzy drinks? How unusual. Well, a milk shake then. No arguing now. I *insist*." And with that, Demelza gripped tight on to Allie and propelled her towards a table outside the café.

As Allie was marched past a phone box, she was sure she caught a glimpse of Gran on the phone, but as she turned to look Demelza Python shoved her into a seat beside a large, overflowing litter bin. Allie found herself firmly wedged between the smelly litter bin and Demelza Python. She wasn't sure which was worse.

But suddenly she saw something much nastier than the bin or Demelza. Ernest Python.

He was creeping towards the canal. He was carrying a large fish, a long stick with a wire loop and a long, narrow sack. Allie went pale. She could guess what they were for.

"I want a double-strawberry ice-cream with nuts and chocolate topping, two

flakes and extra sprinkles," Arabella was
telling Demelza.

"Of course, darling Arabella. And a
milk shake for Allie too." Demelza looked
at Allie. "No need to look so upset. What
a strange child. Doesn't like milk shakes
either. I'll get you a small lolly." Demelza
heaved herself out of her seat and
squeezed past Arabella. Allie waited until
Demelza was safely inside the café, then

she shoved her way out past Arabella.

"Oi! Come back!" shouted Arabella, but Allie was gone.

Allie scanned the canal bank for Ernest Python. There was no sign of him. She ran from one boat to the next, looking between them.

Then Allie saw a flash of orange. Ernest Python was bending down and was half hidden between two boats. He was struggling with something on the canal bank. Allie crept forward to see what it was. It was a long, wet crocodile-shaped sack.

Allie was too late. Ernest Python had captured the crocodile.

Chapter 11

"LEAVE MY CROCODILE alone!" Allie charged full speed at Ernest Python. Ernest Python swung round just as Allie launched herself at him. She had aimed to push him into the canal, but Ernest Python was surprisingly strong. He grabbed hold of Allie and pushed her back.

"Aha. So you *do* have a crocodile . . . I knew you did . . . well, *I've* got it now," puffed Ernest as he tried to stop Allie tripping him up. If anyone had seen Allie and Ernest at that moment they would have thought they were practising some strange dance. Allie pushed Ernest further

back towards the water, then Ernest shifted round and pushed Allie back.

This might have gone on for a while if Ernest had not trodden on the crocodile's tail. Ernest Python knew that if you put a crocodile in a sack they keep very still. Ernest thought that was because crocodiles were stupid, but Ernest was wrong. Crocodiles in sacks keep still because they are listening and waiting until someone comes close. Then they hit them with their tail. Very hard.

THWAP! The crocodile's tail hit Ernest Python like a bat hitting a ball. And like a very odd-shaped ball Ernest Python flew up into the air and curved down gracefully towards the canal. SPLASH!

This was quickly followed by a second SPLASH! The crocodile had suddenly lost his balance and he toppled off the edge of the bank into the canal. He sank like a stone.

Just then Allie heard something strange.

"Nee nah, nee nah!" At first she thought it was Ernest Python wailing in the water, but it got louder and louder.

"Nee nah, nee nah, whoop whoop WHOOOOP." A police car screeched to a halt behind her. To Allie's amazement, Gran got out, followed by three policemen. Gran ran to the side of the canal and pointed at Ernest Python, who suddenly let out a shrill shriek and disappeared under the water.

"That's him!" she cried. "He had a body in a sack. He was throwing it in the canal."

"Right, madam. Leave this with us," said the biggest policeman. "Jump in and arrest that man," he said to the youngest policeman.

"What me, Sarge? Jump in there, Sarge?"

"Yes, you. In there. Jump!" said Sarge. The young policeman held his nose, closed his eyes and jumped.

A few minutes later a dripping Ernest Python and a dripping young policeman sat in the back of the police car. Ernest Python had on a shiny new pair of handcuffs, which looked much smarter than the rusty bed spring he had got stuck on his foot when he'd hit the bottom of the canal. His white, knobbly knees knocked together, as Ernest had somehow managed to lose his trousers.

A large crowd of people had gathered round. Allie noticed Demelza and Arabella at the back. They were trying to see what was going on, but everybody wanted to talk to Sarge.

"Yes, I saw him. Horrible man. He had a big sack. Pushed it into the canal . . ."

"It was definitely a body . . ."

"I saw it move . . ."

Sarge got out his notebook and wrote it all down while Ernest Python shivered in the panda car.

Then, just as Demelza and Arabella had at last managed to push their way through to the front of the crowd, Sarge got into the police car. He switched on the flashing blue light and Demelza peered into the car. Ernest waved damply with his handcuffed hands and Demelza screamed.

"Ernie! What have you *done*?"

Sarge heard the scream and decided his siren sounded better. "Nee nah, nee nah, WHOOOOP." The police car shot off towards the road, closely followed by a yelling Demelza and a wailing Arabella.

It was then that the police frogmen arrived.

Chapter 12

"WHERE IS HE, Allie? What's happened
to him?" Gran looked very worried. The
frogmen were busy throwing themselves
into the canal and Gran had a feeling
that it would be best if they did not find
the crocodile.

"He's still in that horrible sack, Gran. In
the canal. He'll drown . . ." Allie told her.
Gran gasped.

"I've got to get to him, quick, before
those frogmen do." Allie started to
run towards the *Daisy May* which she
had spotted further down the
towpath.

Gran looked confused. "But, Allie, where are you going?"

"I'm going to get my mask and snorkel, Gran. This time I want to be able to see under the water." Allie tore along the towpath. All she could think about was the crocodile lying on the bottom of the canal, trapped in a sack, while the police frogmen swam towards him. She *must* find him first. She *must* get to him before he drowned.

Allie reached the *Daisy May*, jumped

aboard and slipped on a large pool of water. She bumped into the cabin door and slid into the little kitchen to find the floor covered in a trail of muddy water. Allie followed the trail. It led to her cabin. She slowly pushed open the door and there he was. The crocodile was lying on the bottom bunk.

"Oh!" gasped Allie. "You're safe! I can't believe it. Are you all right?"

The crocodile didn't answer. He was fast asleep. Allie sat beside him and put her arms around him, she felt so happy to see him again. Then she noticed something caught between his teeth – a large piece of orange cloth. There was no mistaking Ernest Python's trousers. Allie started giggling and suddenly she couldn't stop. She laughed and laughed and laughed. The crocodile woke up.

"Afternoon," he said. "What's all that noise?"

"Ernest Python's trousers!" spluttered Allie. "*You* caught *him*!"

"Ah. Got a bit carried away after two days with no fish. He reminded me of one of my favourite fish back home. Couldn't bring myself to eat him though. Smelt like a dead lizard."

Allie chuckled. Then she remembered the sack. "But how did you manage to escape?" she asked.

"Crocodile school. Year three. Use of tail in sack. Nearly missed that lesson. Late back from the dentist. Good thing I made it, eh?"

"Yes." Allie smiled. "It's a really good thing you made it."

The crocodile gave a big yawn and closed his eyes. "Back to sleep now," he muttered.

Allie sat beside him and cuddled him until Gran arrived.

*

It was a beautiful, sunny evening as the *Daisy May* chugged far away from the café, the police frogmen and the empty crocodile sack. The frogmen had found the empty sack and Ernest Python had been allowed to leave the police station. Demelza had told him that she never wanted to see a canal again and had taken Arabella straight home.

The crocodile woke up. He flopped off the bottom bunk and wandered out into the evening sunshine.

"Hello, dear," said Gran. "Are you feeling better now?"

"Yes, thank you, Gran," replied the crocodile. His eyes opened wide. "Is that a bucket of fish, Gran?"

Gran smiled. "I had a word with the cook at the café, dear. The police closed the café while they searched the canal. She had a lot of fish and no one to eat it, so I thought you wouldn't want to see perfectly good fish go to waste."

"Certainly not, Gran," agreed the crocodile.

Five cod, three skate and a haddock later, Allie and the crocodile were splashing around in the canal. Allie sat on the crocodile as he glided along in the water beside the *Daisy May*. Gran sat at the helm and smiled. At last their holiday had begun.